*For God so loved the world
that he gave his only begotten
that whosoever believeth in him
should not perish, but have everlasting life.
~John 3:16*

Love and Salt
Prison Sentence
Gates of Hell
The Poet
9mm
Seasons of Love
Brokenhearted Memories
Dare
Tomorrow Becomes Yesterday
Destination
Berry Best
Glassware
Lovely Love
Ballad Of The Lonely Man
To My Sweetheart
True Man
Son of David
Forever Young
Touched
Man On The Wall
Minutes Go By
For Nevin
The Plight
A Soldier's Perspective
Shining Light
Soldier's Grave
Candlelight
Warrior Maiden

Man With No Name
A Work
Clock Has Struck
Words Not Written
Love's Eternal Bond
A Love Verse
Time
Listen To The Sound
I Pray Today
Strangers
Demon of Death
Angel of Death
You Never Saw Me
Let It Play Out
Burst of Colors
Tears In My Hand
Beast In Me
Abiding Still
One True Friend
Great God
RIP
My Soulless Walks
Lost Without Your Love
Eternal Sheets
My Bestest Friend
Bed
Mind
Ace Replaced

Daeh
Huh?
My Partner
My Boy
Puppet Clown
Crying Soul
Cry To God
Fellowman
Poetry
Life
Fill Me
If It Was Love
Missing Him
A Pain Exists
Simple Truth
Missin' You
Out There
Alphabet Caper
Dear Uncle Dave
Rambles
A Prayer
Flame
Sunken Canoe
The Cost
Naked There
Lonely Void
Eighty Eight
Imagination

Feeling
The Father's Love
Old Self
Nature
Lord I pray
The River
Operation Tryst
Post Shout
Love Potion
Words In My Head
Future Make
Unbleached
Mister Sinister
Walk it onto the Page
Inherent Vice
Inside My Head
Pair of Eyes
Silver and Knowledge
Port
Sweeter 'n Sweet Tea
Very Extremely Pretty
Words
The Maddening Hive
More Than Winds Blow
Ink and Quire
Little Anna Marie
Jack and Jill
Happy Writing

LOVE AND SALT

Love and salt
are two things
I can't live without
well I guess if I had to
maybe I could
but of that I have utmost doubt.

PRISON SENTENCE
Some say life is a prison
I'm not sure I reckon that's true
but either way
I know night and day
I want to spend my sentence
with you.

GATES OF HELL

Fire rose from atop the mountain
as he walked through the valley
toward the gates of hell
the kiss of her love
lay fresh on his lips
as she died while wishing him well
demons had come
to take her away
ferrying her soul to hell
so her man walks to the fiery gates
his is the story I tell
the fiends then launched their arrows
as alone he raised his shield
and although a thousand volleys
the man refused to yield
in a world beyond earth and water
where the sun dare show no face
he fought from a heart of eternal love
to save her from this terrible place
the battle raged for a time unknown
as he fought with unbreakable faith
so the devil himself
rose out of his chair
that he may see his face
a soul once in hell
may never be freed
unless it can be replaced

so the man and the devil
struck hands in a deal
her eternity for his
he would trade
released from her shackles
through the gates she walked
as tears from her eyelids fell-
the kiss of his love
lay fresh on her lips
as he smiled and wished her well
then turned unafraid
and walked away
into the gates of hell.

THE POET

Beautiful evil
loomed ore his heart
before violently taking control
from fingers fed
once blood now ink
he writes to save his soul
within his mind
feeds the devil's legion
inside imprisoned thrive
so write he must
to free the beast
a verse to stay alive
locked inside an eternal prison
through bars he peers from his eyes
although comprised of flesh and blood
in truth the demon's disguise
whiskey and drugs
shan't dim nor mane
his everlasting affliction of perpetual pain
churning words to verse
in an everlasting hell
his deepest fears smiling
while wishing him well
a life of eternal torment
eternity times eternity
times seven
a tattered spirit

forced to write
in the hopes of glimpsing heaven
an unfortunate fool
this soul
that bears many a name
the poet
the man
the woman
the damned
this creature born in pain.

9MM

Was it the seven point six two's
that took his friends
forcing their souls silent be?
or were they dead already
from battles within
those bullets
setting them free
this question he begs
in hopes that the pain
within his soul
he finally may quell
sadly the truth
no answer exists
save reality
he cannot leave hell
living
dead
the silhouette soldier
salutes
as he sings his last song
broken heart
beats the drum
for his brothers marking time
the soldiers marched on
all alone save his demons
surrounded by stones
bearing witness

to the silent below
on the ground
poured whiskey
says hello to his brothers
laughing as the tears finally flow
hating himself for being the one
forced to witness them go
nothing left but memories
which soon the wind will blow
save the color of red
splayed naked
on Iraqi sand and Afghan snow
there are faces those
who've truly seen war
faces those who have not
those who've not
cannot ever see
that the man who tastes
the taint of war
taints the taste
of feeling free
for the sounds of battle
never cease
at war he forever will be
from tattered bag he pulls
the grantor of his release
the ferryman
who asks no questions

offering an exit
which perhaps offers peace
his final thought
was of what people would say
when they lay him
in the dirt with his friends
the answer to their question
causes a smile to form
finally
together again
out of love for his countrymen
he swore an oath
exchanging his youth for a rifle
only to find
silent screams replace peace
see children the bombs stifle
the only luxury afforded
were the sisters and brothers
beside him at his three
his six and his nine
but as fate would have it
in the name of freedom
they too he would bury in time
the next question imposed
perhaps not from your head
still are words I've heard said
referring to veteran's suicide dead
"Are they not selfish,

for not wanting to live?"
The real question is—
...how much more
do we demand
that they give?
was it the nine
mike mike
that took his life
forcing his heart
silent be
or was he dead already
from battles within
that bullet
setting him free?
lines before leaving
lines I must give
addressed to the veterans
to those who still live
far too many of us
on a daily basis
share the same fate
as the man in this play
he's as real
or as fake
as you allow him to be
but he doesn't have to be you
he doesn't have to be me
if the pain is too hard

from the terror and shards
bloody nightmares awaken
pulse racing
hands shaking heavy
heart needing
I urge you my friend
use paper and pen
to sop your soul's heavy bleeding
if you decide you're worth
more dead than alive
weighed all the options
found no will to survive
the pain held too tight
left you lonely and blind
just know pulling that trigger
leaves an empty you
a broken family behind
for we are true family
us veterans who live
but what strength is our bond
if support we don't give
to those who've stopped fighting
because it hurts just to live
a lifetime of demons
I could write volumes on pain
but wallowing in hurt
only makes you insane
if your finger's on the trigger

and you feel the need to pull
know we don't think you weak
nor do we think you a fool
in any way
but leaving like this
leaves the demons to stay
to burden and plague us all
giving them roam
in our darkest hour
causing another to fall
no my friend
I cannot stop you
and shall salute
should you
bid us farewell
but know
if you stay
we can fight them together this day
and send those demons to hell.

Every hour and a half a veteran commits suicide.

If you're a veteran or service member in crisis, please dial **988 then Press 1** or text **838255**

SEASONS OF LOVE

Time will pass
seasons change
winter turns to spring
you'll never know the love I have
or what to me you bring
the sun will come
the snow then melts
the grass and flowers show
and like the roots beneath the ground
my love for you will grow
pass of winter
pass of spring
summer shows its face
the love I have for you is true
and time cannot erase
a summer night
the moon is full
the stars come out to play
and if I had three life times
no words in them could say
the love I've felt
the love I have
the love for you today
good times and summer
come and gone
fall weather in the air
I wish that with each season pass

you'd know how much I care
the way you walk
the way you smile
I love everything that's you
for love I'd give you everything
I only wish you knew
when you're gone for but a day
it feels like eternity
without your love its emptiness
you're everything to me
fall is gone
winter's here
darkness slowly creeps
I'll say it baby one last time
I love you
now I sleep.

BROKENHEARTED MEMORIES

When I first received the news
"You're having a little boy"
no words can describe
the happiness I felt
as my soul was filled with joy
I remember our conversations
as you slowly started to grow
my mind was filled with stories
and the places we would go
so many choices
from toys to names
I could see you running
as we played little games
I loved you so
so much
I thought my heart would break
how can there be a loving God?
starting to give
but only to take?
I felt your little heartbeat
as you whispered
near my heart
he took my little prince charming
leaving me to scream in the dark
each day your heart grew stronger
until the day it ceased
leaving me with empty nights

without love
joy
or peace
the nights that bring me happiness
are foggy with the pain
when I dream that we are holding hands
as I softly whisper your name
my resolve is to be stronger
when I hear or say your name
until I see a smiling baby
and it rushes in again
I hear you whisper
in the wind
I see you in the sky
my knees go weak
my heart turns cold
and my cry begins to cry
people ask me how I feel
they say it will all be fine
why then do I feel this pain
who would take what's only mine?
they tell me they know how I feel
if I need to talk
they'll always be my friend
they know nothing of the pain I feel
all I want is my little boy
his heart to beat again
I know we'll be together again

holding hands
in a world far away
there is no comfort
for I need you now
I want you back today
my arms were made
for holding you
and that was stripped away
no words describing how I feel
if there was I could not say
they took my tiny
precious boy
gave me ashes in return
making dust
out of heart and soul
hope and dreams in a little urn
I try to find the words to write
as my hand goes limp
to match my blackened heart
alone I sit
a broken vessel
of stress
full of loss
as my soul goes dark
all I have is memories
with little left to give
with each day as a struggle
to find the will to live

I know you live within my heart
I'll see you some sweet day
but tonight
I am lost and lonely
with nothing left to say.
-*For, Star. A friend and beautiful soul.*

DARE

Dare to dream and be branded a fool
dare to inspire or break the rules
dare to be free and risk losing it all
dare to rebel and head for a fall
dare to imagine
risk standing alone
follow ideals
risk having no home
dare to be different
and dare to think
dare to stand or fall over the brink
dare to inspire
and others you'll lead
risk falling in love
for your heart to bleed
dare to have strength
to climb higher peaks
while possessing humility
to help those who are weak
acquire a love
for all living things
keep a song in your soul
for your lips to sing
dare to believe and do all you can
to bring light and color
into a barren land
when evil is present

and all remain silent
dare to be the one to speak
be strong unwavering
powerful and firm
while remaining humble and meek
when all others leave
be the one to stay
assuring that wrong is set right
so that the young and the old
the sickly and weak
may sleep soundly in bed at night
dare to be different
to have a voice
stand against fear and hate
dare to reach out
give a helping hand
dare and dare to be great.

TOMORROW BECOMES YESTERDAY

The piano plays
so turn the page
before tomorrow
becomes yesterday
play on piano
please if you may
while here we sit
and listen today
breath in the beauty
before the time's past
for even the lily
will not always last
and life always seems to be
moving too fast
there's music above
in the sparkling rain
though not as sweet
as when I taste your name
again I fear I've fallen in love
and for that
my heartless heart's to blame
live in this moment just you and I
betwixt the perfect picture
of earth and skies
almost as perfect
as what I see
in your eyes

so please dance with me love
this moment is ours
to remember forever
as we vibe with the stars
while the moon
ever resting
smiling above
serves as a witness
to our eternal love
there's no promise of tomorrow
nor the rest of today
but I truly wish
that tonight you'll stay
until our tomorrow
becomes yesterday.

DESTINATION

The light is fading faster
and darkness creeps on in
I see a great big hole
and I know I'm falling in
no one ever warned me
of this hellish hole
and so I wasted my life away
and sold the devil my soul
I thought I loved the devil
I thought he was my friend
but now I see that fire
is all I get in the end
I cannot save my own soul
no matter how hard I try
so all that's left to do
is drink my last dollar and die
but suddenly I heard a voice
and saw a hand reaching down
I felt myself being lifted up
up to higher ground
the hand it placed me on a hill
and oh the sights I did see
that hell hole underneath
but mansions above me
then I heard him talking
He was speaking to me
He said which will you choose

that hell hole or me?
I wanted to open my mouth and say
yes of course I do
but suddenly I realized
I am you the reader
and the choice is up to you.

BERRY BEST

Don't change a word my friend
heaven or hell be damned
please don't change
my happy cowlick strand
close eyes
say prayers
stay kids in the sand
and when we grow up
we'll always be together
my berry best
soul land
the unplanned
and wherever you are
in whatever land
I'll always love you
my savior
my un-damned
unknown to them
you or me
without you
I can't see
I love you so much
I believe you're
my sanctuary
fairy
one reprieve
my tender

loving smile
the heart
on life's sleeve
my light
my darkness
to you
I'll always cleave.

GLASSWARE

Imagine with me if you will
giant glassware crashing down
more of a cliff than a hill
it tumbles and smashes
itsy bitsy shattered shards
marring holes
gouging scars
not one whole piece
made it down the mount
just a glassy mist
battered adrift out to sea
that shattered mist was me
then a warrior appears
though not of thin air
a familiar face
the lady so fair
my glass became whole
with her standing there
for the first time in centuries
I breathed a breath of free air
in her arms
all my atoms
flood with light
when I think of her
my all is filled
with love
in all its might

gold and tatters
jewels and shatters
with her
I find none of it matters
only her
sailing without compass
on the eternal starlit sea
no watch no worries
only love without hurry
where she is
there too is my home
and no matter the distance
battle rattle or instance
I've her love
so I'm never alone
for this gift of love
from The Creator above
I'm eternally
forever indebted
for if I'd had to wager
if her love would me favor
on myself
I'd never have betted.

LOVELY LOVE

Oh lovely love
happy love
where have you gone?
why have you flown away?
it goes without saying
but I'll say it to say it
I really wish you had stayed.

BALLAD OF THE LONELY MAN

It's so lonely I can't breathe
even with faith I don't believe
no happier skies
no soon reprieve
you failed to listen
or understand what I wrote
along with all the people I love the most
none can help me and so
I succumb to my woe as the lonely ghost
so strike the lights
mister boatman we can go
from the day I was born
I shoulda known
bounced check in hand
I'm just a one way ticket
to a one man show
I've too much color
to live in black and white
too much love in my soul
to harbor hatred or strife
but you've made me sign a receipt
for love that I gave
to make me a slave
an even though I'm still kickin
this don't feel like livin
having to pay dearly
for any love that I'm givin

so strike the lights
mister boatman we can go
from the day I was born
I shoulda known
bounced check in hand
I'm just a one way ticket
to a one man show
on a fiery freight train
bound for a place I don't know
cuz all I know is
I'm slave to a lonely heart
a one way ticket to a one man show
I thought this time would be different
thought I'd finally found a home
but only to discover
with you I'm alone
I don't know why
the ones we love
can hurt us so
but if with you is home
and home is a prison
then where on earth do I go?
if only with you I can be?
but a convict you can't see
I don't know what words to say
or what actions to show
the only thing I know is that it seems to me
I've been dealt the one man ticket

to a packed out lonely
one man show
so strike the lights
mister boatman
we can go
from the day I was born
I shoulda known
bounced check in hand
I'm just a one way ticket
to a one man show
on a freight
bound for a place I don't know
cuz all I know is
I've been bound to a lonely heart
but at least loneliness loves me
wherever I go
making sure that I know
I'm just a one way ticket to a one man show.

<u>TO MY SWEETHEART</u>
I love your eyes
I love your laugh
I love the way you smile
and even when I'm gone for days
you're with me all the while
when we kiss I lose me breath
sends tingles down my spine
with my tongue so gently
on you draw a line
buttons loose
the music soft
the clothes fall to the floor
then I take you at my will
against the bathroom door
your head falls back
your hair falls loose
I lay you on the bed
I smile call you sweetheart
and kiss you on your head
I hold your body gently
but firmly have control
you are the secret to my heart
the key that locks my soul
for you I'm filled with passion
none else could satisfy
I'll be there with you when you laugh
I'll hold you when you cry

our breathing quickens
drenched in sweat
we both then reach the peak
you gasp and roll back on the bed
both our body's weak
I wrap my arms around you
kiss you on the cheek
I hold you tight and snuggle close
then we fall asleep.

TRUE MAN

What makes a man?
is it strength and power
or the clothing that he wears
places he attends
involved in uppity affairs
is it in his money
or possessions he's obtained
peer group
job
location
or is it in his name
now some of these things matter
and some of them are true
and what these words are saying
isn't something new
a true man starts with inner self
his heart his soul and mind
and yes he should be strong and tough
but also meek and kind
a true man is about sacrifice
himself he freely gives
to make the world a better place
that is why he lives
this man can take a lover's heart
and put it in a place
where nothing ever harms it
and love it till he breaks

this man will fight for loved ones
protect and serve till death
and he will always be there
until his ending breath
love and truth
compassion
strength
and faith
and then
sacrifice and serving
are some things which make a man.

SON OF DAVID

The proverbs of Solomon
son of David king of Israel
a man after God's own heart
destroyer of giants
and writer of psalms
prayers that we may not depart
let us receive
the instruction
of wisdom
justice and judgment
and equity
knowledge and discretion
with strength and honor
to deliver enslaved from depression
understand the proverb
the interpretation
the words of the wise
and their dark sayings
to be listening
tread holy
not stumbling braying
and if sinners entice we
consent let us not
for we are bought with a price
with them we shan't cast a lot
for their feet run to evil
their hands shed innocent blood

so we refrain from their path
or risk the fiery flood
and a soul drowned in crud.

FOREVER YOUNG

Youth isn't forever we know
but it also is you see
for all of us
are all as young
as we will ever be
some people feel anger
at themselves and or others
for their youth
believe they wasted
but then on pasts
their present they spend
meaning true loss
they've only just tasted
youth isn't forever we know
but it also is you see
for all of us are all as young
as we will ever be.

TOUCHED

All I want to do is touch you
all I want is to hold your hand
too dangle our feet in the water
to make love with you in the sand
to draw you a bath light some candles
and gently caress your sweet face
then as you lie there in the bed
take your body
secure it gently with lace
I will tie the knots so gently firm
and your body will be at my will
for when I'm alone with you baby
I love the emotions I feel
your hair falls loose on your body
I'm in love from your hair to your toes
I want to hold you
and bite your neck gently
and kiss you on the end of your nose
when I'm with you I'm a hopeless romantic
hanging on to every word that you say
I want to quit all I do and do nothing
so I can be with you all of each day
I look in your eyes and I'm peaceful
the passion and love I see there
I thought I was happy as single
until I saw you standing there
now that you're gone I feel empty

alone by myself in the night
you were my pillar of strength
my beautiful beacon of light
we are separated by countries and water
by oceans and time we're apart
but no matter how great of a distance
you hold the keys to my heart
I stare at your picture for hours
and dream of the times that we had
then reality tells me you're gone
I feel nothing but empty and sad
please return to me baby
please hold my hand once more
I've opened my heart to you darling
I beg you to enter the door
I want to carry you through the hard times
be there to help lift your load
to always have you with me
I'll hold you and
make one set of prints in life's road
you have my love and affection
baby you make me complete
and until I tell you how I feel
I will never be able to sleep
so tonight as I stare in the heavens
and wish on a beautiful star
I wonder what it is that your thinking
and how I wish I knew were you are

food has lost its taste
colors are all turned to gray
and things that used to matter
about them I have nothing to say
the life I thought I had
is beginning to fall apart
and I cannot keep on moving
with this great empty hole in my heart
I hope you are getting my letters
I pray you read this one tonight
for I will always love you sweetheart
you are all that is good and right.

MAN ON THE WALL

The life had long since fled his eyes
succeeded by a ghastly decadence
if portrayed by a smell
maggot infested feces shrouded in rotten corpse
I pause before his harrowing face
reciprocating me in trident like gaze
mind escaping my soul cries out
"why keep tormenting unrelenting oppression
as though watching me drown is your only obsession?"
….He replies with a smirk
to my rhetorical question
'tis tenfold misery
times tenfold
having love
knowing he loved the same
opposition infallible
now inane we cause pain
this perpetual notion
the other's to blame
as we wallow in mud
'neath a torrent of shame
for self-preservation
we fought from within
howbeit unknowing
that neither can win
for this man in the mirror

the man on the wall
is the demon's reflection that inhabits us all
living inside yet I am his slave
even if life it was me who him gave
how can I conquer
thus reclaiming control?
by re-claiming as master my own heart and soul?
but my mind soon unchecked
again runs away
now I'm the man on the wall
with the trident like gaze
staring at me
as I'm staring
staring at me today.

MINUTES GO BY

It was ten in the night
and with no hope in sight
he sat there beside her
as she lost the fight for life
the doctor said it was bad
and no one he'd ever had
had ever recovered
from something like this
so he asked him to leave
and fell down on his knees
and he prayed God above
to please send him some love tonight
for he can't go through life
without his beautiful wife
he loves so much
a brother walks down the aisle
he has to force a smile
or a little laugh
he sees his brother
in the coffin
the smile on his face
in his mind he can't erase
he's down the aisle
the minutes pass
the memories
they went too fast
the times they spent

they worked and played
it all seems like a dream
or just yesterday
and as the tears flow down his face
he can't find
the words to say
the husband mourning
he starts to weep
as his wife enters
eternal sleep
in the adjoining room
a mother cries
when she hears her child's
about to die
her twelve year old daughter
has an hour left to live
now she sobs about the love
that she can't ever give
the brother stands
beside the grave
he feels a slave
to this pain
and as the tears flow down his face
he still can't find
the words to say
and the minutes go by
time it goes
where it starts and ends

nobody knows
people come
people go
and all we have
are their memories to show
love for a day
love for a year
keep your loved ones very near
say I love you
say I care
show your affection everywhere
say I love you tonight.

FOR NEVIN

The old cemetery down the hollow
sadly I know it well
for its home to some of my family
and a different kind of hell
eyes blurry reach for the bottle
it's a long road to hell
but I'm on full throttle
maybe I outta jot a last thought
on my cigarette box I know it's tox-
-ic but I can't quit minds sick heart's trying to quit
Lord knows we can't take another hit
my souls licked'n laid out on fentanyl
damn it all take out my shooter
it's my life my call
pistol to the head'n
wanting to end to it all
the peace of the dead
the only separation is a little piece of lead
then strikes the dread on my son's face
a few pounds of pressure a big decision
then I see their faces
in visions with such precision
it alters my conviction
filling my suicidal mind with contradiction
giving death thoughts eviction
a family man dad
my new life mission-

brother father grandma
gone in a year and I miss 'em
I can't write call or kiss 'em
and the pain's my mind messing
but a sobriety cloak
is the new suit I'm wearing
left the bike club swearing
to give my family extra love
and each day's a brand new
same ole struggle
a tug-a
war
but I take strength in knowing
on my demons
I can close the door
and when they climb in the window
a sober fist I'll show'em
damn them all
send 'em back to hell
and say goodnight
then hold my loved ones tight-
life's a real tough fight
but with a little love
it'll be alright.
keep the good goals in sight
stay the course with all my might
over wrong be choosin right
in the valley of darkness be a light

until the mountain height
and sun of love shines bright
until then I soldier on
on my lips I got a song I sing
of all the love I'm bout to bring
cuz I was twelve rounds past twelve
facefirst down for the count
but God didn't count me out
give a shout to the self fears
without a doubt
I've been through worse before
fire charred fields
and shipwrecked shores
so I know I can handle
tumultuous weather
an when it's all belly up
it's my choice to make it better
burying my closest family was
my soul ripped though my heart
it's a pain that's blacker than black
a seemingly eternal dark
a nightmarish song
yet to get love
first love
so I pick up the pieces and sail on
because only love is endless
and this night will have a dawn.

THE PLIGHT

A transaction and handshake
the deal is made
like a game of chess
the pawn's been played
the cat the mouse
the rabbit run
the hawk is out
wants food and fun
wars are started
wars are fought
wars are won and lost
it's the pawns who without question
will pay the ultimate cost
they will live
they will laugh
smile love and cry
again the player moves a piece
another pawn will die
lawyers lie and win in court
politicians with scripts recite
sick and twisted comedy
narrating this terrible plight
why can't we live together in love
when will there ever be peace?
when people can live without fear
children smile and peacefully sleep

some claim to have the answers
some say a truce can be reached
but it's all just words
and all still absurd
for it's lies
they're using to teach
extorting money to hear themselves screech
so much hate and contention
in the sky
and air we breath
we wake and feel its heavy weight
for us there's no reprieve
maybe there is no answer
no end to the advancement of wrong
which would mean then
it's kinda pointless to write
for there's no end to this pitiful song.

A SOLDIER'S PERSPECTIVE
I see the crosses
white and bare
against the evening sky
then ask myself the question
why did they have to die?
what is war
what is death
why must there be this pain?
I'm given the order to kill
and I don't even know their names
I look at myself and the enemy
and realize how much we're alike
we both are serving a cause
both locked in someone else's fight
and so as I raise my weapon
be first to shoot them down
witnessing the life blood flowing
pooling on the ground
I ask another question
before I walk away
why must there be wars
why am I here today?
how can I hate a man
who wears the same shoes as me
perhaps both of us are blind
and the people cannot see
we do not fight for country

but only to survive
and so we use our weapons
to take each others lives
and as I raise my gun
and the trigger I then pull
it leaves me feeling empty
alive to live a fool
so it's not with hate but love
as a tear falls from my heart
I leave his dying body
and then my soul goes dark
and all the taxpayers
especially Americans
in this tale played a valuable part.

SHINING LIGHT

Why is there anger
when there should be peace
why am I awake
when I should be asleep
the words keep on coming
and beg me to write
and so my fingers keep moving
long into the night
the words have always lived
and I write nothing new
but now they have asked me
to show them to you
so this all has been written
as I know you agree
I do not know why
they have chosen to use me
I must keep living
and hope a light I can shine
but these words are their own
they never were mine
do not give up yet
because tomorrow will come
and something great
can happen before you are done
life can be twisted
full of questions and mystery
it gives us character

and that or lack
is what makes history
all people possess greatness
but some refuse to show
and that is a sadness
that they will never know
living each moment
and loving till it hurts
can be the greatest thing you do
while feeling like the worst
you cannot judge yourself
by actions others have done
it is your life you judge
and your song will be sung
so before you give up
and walk into the night
remember it can be you
who is the world's shining light.

SOLDIER'S GRAVE

The soldier writhes
upon the ground
the guns above
make awful sound
he holds her picture
near his chest
he thinks of her
and perfect rest
the way his hand
would clasp with hers
his eyelids close
it turns to blur
his mind goes back
to time and day
when last he heard
his baby say
I love you
he holds her picture
in his hand
while dying there
upon the sand
he gave his life
his love his wife
for "freedom's cause"
to "end a strife"
across the world
his loved one lays

and wonders how
he is today
but never again
will she feel his heart
or have him hold her
in the dark
he breaths I love you
with his last breath
the picture falls
he enters death
the music plays
she walks the aisle
the tears have come
he has a smile
she holds his flag
against her chest
they lower him
to be at rest
the people come
but then they go
the time will come
and none will know
the sacrifice
that both them gave
or the significance
of a soldier's grave.

CANDLELIGHT

I lay awake
staying up
all night
just a pen and paper
by the candlelight
but all I could see
was her sweet face
and the way she moved
with perfect grace
she is so perfect
and so right
from her hair
down to her toes
I'm so in love
but am so low
because she doesn't know
I try to tell her
but I can't
I know I'm not for her
the tears now block my vision
and everything is blurred
the kind of love
I have for her
is perfect this I know
because I love her so much
I had to let her go
she deserves

much more than me
the world and
then some more
and so I back out softly
and close heart's little door
I stare at pictures of us
and tears
well in my eye
in the breeze I feel her
I see her in the sky
whenever
I would see her
my heart would beat so fast
all those feelings that I had
I hope will always last
whenever she would touch me
on the hand or on the arm
I would melt
like candle wax
beneath her gentle charm
she had blonde hair
eyes of blue
her voice was soft and slow
all I ever did
was love
and now she'll never know
I put on my suit
my watch and tie

take flowers from the vase
then I seal this letter
with her favorite lace
the letter is short but with love
this is how it reads-
I love you baby
always have
there are no words
to say
how much
that I love you
forever and a day -
I am so sorry
I was not there
to catch you
at the fall
or there
to hold you gently
as you gave your final call
I never
got to kiss you
I'm sorry now I know
I never should have left
never let you go
I seal this letter
with a kiss
a teardrop hits the note
because now

she'll never read it
everything I wrote
I place the flowers
in the coffin
the letter
in her hand
my heart goes cold
my knees give way
and now it hurts to stand
I look at her
all I feel
remorse regret
and hate
because I never told her
now it is too late
the music stops
they close the lid
there's nothing left to say
one last tear
I wipe my eyes
and then
I walk away.

WARRIOR MAIDEN

Atop the rock
aloft a silvery lake
personifying
colossal resolve
veins of ink
in blood's stead from the heart
clenching her staff
stood the solus lupus
a warrior maiden
to ward off the dark
one eye on grandeur
the other toward
tempests reposed
she gazed straight ahead
a luminary beacon
and utterance of reason
betwixt the living
and the literary dead
although some believe her
to be mythical creature
and others
attesting her existence
claim them wrong
they twain
avow a family relation
and equal admiration
for mother

their warrior maiden
a beacon of light
for verse lost her life
now through ink
she forever lives on
a literary paragon
through the soul of the writer
manifested
through poetry and song.

THE MAN WITH NO NAME

I believe in peace and yet
I join the ranks to fight the war
I understand purpose and duty
so I say goodbye to mom and shut the door
I now have a rifle in place of a pen
becoming a number instead of a name
I see all the evil that man can create
all of the violence
love replaced with hate
how can this evil be done in the name of peace?
so that those who cannot fight
have a safe place to sleep?
some call me a murderer
other's a saint
how people feel
are the pictures they paint
they'll tell you what they are
but not what they ain't
I do not have an answer
to war's evil face
none of the images can ever be replaced
what I do know is this
that soldiers want peace
because it is them
who have no place to sleep
I carry a rifle so that "others can live"
even if my life in the end I must give

all have opinions few take action
words full of hate
a justice retraction
but of course you cannot know
unless you see war
tell your mother goodbye
and then shut the door
put on your boots and stare death in the face
living the images that time can't erase
soldiers are needed
we taxpayers pay for war
and so I must go
even if the answers I may never know
I pray in the end that peace is obtained
even when I'm forgotten or blamed
the soldier
the number
the man with no name.

A WORK

I search for words within my soul
to tell me what is real
but there is no answer
for the nothingness I feel
I close my eyes and hold my breath
just let my feelings go
it's then I ask the questions
to which I'll never know
it's by the water I find peace
to still my wanting heart
to find myself
become as one
and fade into the dark
walk on water walk on glass
walk on clouds of air
then to face reality
where the demons stare
angels of fire
angels of death
angels of spite and hate
where goodness came
and tried to be
but only came too late
gone is love where with it came
but vanished in the night
and only pain and sorrow
with the coming light

some would think that darkness
brings in the hurt and pain
but the light is bright and still
it all rushes in again
and so to write would make no sense
when nothing there to be
but maybe this will have an answer
maybe this is key
to live in nothing
time stands still
existence reel so low
and anything that has a thought
will then it cease to know
close your eyes
close the door
fade into the past
for nothing ever came or went
and nothing ever lasts.

CLOCK HAS STRUCK

Question the man who says
he alone can see God
those who condemn you
who serve a God of hate
will gladly stand by
and pray for your fate
logic and reason are the first to go
when you blindly follow
a reason unknown
stand for reason above all else
for losing your mind
is losing yourself
be weary of those
who tell you not to think
demanding you follow them
over the brink
knowledge is power
without it you'll die
alone with your 'family'
wondering why
be branded a traitor
or be branded a fool
be branded a thinker
or an idealist
a brand they will give
better to be branded
than relinquish the freedom to live

the clock has struck
a decision must be made
be a free thinking you
or crowd loving slave.

WORDS NOT WRITTEN

A note within a stanza
a word within a poem
the emptiness between
has captured my mind
thus warming my soul
unspoken whispers
on blank sheets of paper
torn parchment
blackened
by poets ink
carries her secrets
within the hollow
empty spaces
the secrets I treasure
are those still buried
my favorite song
has never been sung
my favorite poem
not yet written
dear maestro
lead your music
in all its glory
poet
write your moving
and passionate words
with heart and soul
I shall discover their secrets

within the empty spaces
for therein lies
the tears beneath the joy
and the peace amidst the pain
the words I read
are the words unwritten
the music I hear
is the song not sung.

LOVE'S ETERNAL BOND

Death stole her soul
softer than a whisper leaves lips
as she slept in the sands beside the sea
a letter lay within her hand
upon which she'd penned a poem of love
to a man unworthy
of such a noble cause
as teardrops fell
her eyes for eternity closed
as a raging and relentless chill
as the stormy sea within his soul
would cease his beating heart
in fleeting moment
he gasped for air to pen
such loving words as these
for his soul was knit
by eternal love
to that woman who lay by the sea
by her side the angels knelt
as the demons for him did come
but neither angels
nor demons
could fathom
their souls unbreakable love
so the demons lay him
upon the sand
and struck a deal

with the angels above
forever together
their souls un severed
slept they upon the sands by the sea
eternal love
forever unbroken
'tis the love
I have for thee.

A LOVE VERSE

If the places we went
were music I wrote
and our beautiful moments
the magnifical notes
it would be my favorite song
all the flowers you see
are the love we share
and all of our kisses
the clouds in the air
displaying our love to the world
our favorite song
the birds can sing
for they know the love
only you can bring
for you are the song in my soul
the wind whispers softly
as our secrets we share
watching the stars
without worry or care
falling asleep in each others arms
one last kiss before we say goodnight
on a bed of grass in the pale moonlight
you will always be my love.

TIME

Give me your love my dearest friend
ensure I am peaceful be it a bitter end
I've lost track of you again and again
you greatest frenemy to my fellow men
I love you a lot
feel you give me so little
once I felt first
til' you took me to middle
how long before you take me
from the middle to the end?
you've already taken my brother
my one my true
my best friend
I will always love you
and wish you were all mine
tho surely I must hate you
'cuz you're the bastard time.

LISTEN TO THE SOUND

Can you hear that?
the sound of
starving children dying
the sound of elderly dying alone
single mothers and children without a home
it's the sound of the helpless
left to drown
it's the sound of murder and rape
all around
the sound of racism and hate
can you hear it?
can you see?
sights and sounds
of a world that is
that doesn't have to be.

I PRAY TODAY

I stare in heaven to see God's face
Lord Yeshua please my sins erase
Lord God Almighty please send some grace
please free my mind from Satan's hold
till on that day I reach the fold
I failed you much
I left the way
Lord I want to know
to hear you say
"Well done thou good
and faithful servant"
on that glorious day
my faults are many
my strength is weak
but You alone
my God I seek
please cleanse my heart
and guide my way
Lord God
I seek your face today.

STRANGERS

I held her hand
as she suffered upon the bed
my dearest wife
my best friend
she touched my cheek
and whispered final secrets
as I listened
I realized
I had lived a lifetime
with a complete stranger
she said her final words
and the angels carried her away
I walked slowly to the door
turned to take one last look
at my loving wife
my best friend
my heart's home
a final look at the woman
I had never known.

DEMON OF DEATH

I slowly breath so out of breath
I close my eyes and enter death
I see the demons in the night
I'm helpless now I cannot fight
but watch in horror as they take flight
while in a room not square or round
my ears are filled with twisted sound
the demons black they have no face
it's screaming now what is this place?
convulsing why my mind erase
my thoughts are gone it's empty space
I'm in this place be death or hell
the colors twist I cannot tell
I see the faces throughout the spaces
I see a face all by itself
I see it all but not myself
the colors flash all orange and black
convulse again reality back
the end of wars
of death and strife
the end of hell
I'm back to life.

ANGEL OF DEATH

I hear a whisper in my ear
I hear the whisper can you hear?
I close my eyes I'm still as death
I cannot move I'm out of breath
I see the visions death and hate
something so wrong could I create
I've no idea of what I saw
I've no idea I can't recall
the visions flashed or did I die?
what did I see?
I want to cry
I'm as a child all alone
I don't exist I have no home
the visions end
its black then white
I snap to feet regain my sight
the shaking room
I must sit down
it's after me it's all around
is it a demon
angel of death?
I'm shaking now
try'n catch my breath
eternity three seconds passed
suddenly
I'm back at last.

YOU NEVER SAW ME

I saw you last night
you didn't see me
I waved, laughing
yelling- Hey ;)...
but you didn't see me
you turned
and for the briefest
sometimes longer moments
I thought you did
I really thought you did
you brushed past me
I didn't turn this time because
it's a story so old
I already know
even naked alone
behind closed doors
you never saw me.

LET IT PLAY OUT
Life's messy unkind
can leave you feeling maimed
even blind
looking for a rewind
but I think you'll find
in valleys of stress and doubt
take a deep breath or two
and just
let it play out
just let it play out
let the situation
have its bout
laugh cry
scream or pout-
history shows
if you just
let it play out
you'll possibly play less
the losing lass or lout.

BURST OF COLORS

I looked to get lost in her eyes
beautiful eternal sunrise
a palate of all the right notes
and colors
my heart shuddered
voice stuttered
soul sputtered
then all was calm
all was right
as I stood before
the queen of my night
eternal sunlight sunrise
a burst of happy colors
this woman
this Muse
this love like no other.

TEARS IN MY HAND

I've got your tears in my hand
your heart and soul
my promised land
a life without your light
is a life that is damned
a lightless night
a lifeless land
my friend
my friend
I've got your tears in my hand
my friend
my friend
my promised land.

BEAST IN ME

Within me there's a beast
within an empty cage
that's filled with leagues of misery
like pain and wild rage
and no matter
the words I conjure
I'm blank before
the maddening page
and all I see or know and feel
is the beast with its painful rage.

ABIDING STILL

When my work
on earth is done
when the race
on earth I've run
as I lie there in the grave
freed by death
no more a slave
may there be
upon my face
a perfect peace
death can't erase
for I'm at peace
within God's will and
He is with me
abiding still.

ONE TRUE FRIEND

If I looked the whole world over
and then nine times beside
for a friend that was so true
and our friendship could abide
I would never find one as such
oh God
am I asking too much?
there are people all around me
and I've nowhere left to turn
it's like I am the butter
and this ole world's the churn
I've looked and looked forever
and a lot of time has passed
I wonder deep inside my heart
will I find a friend at last?
each day is passing faster
they turn to months to years
my heart is growing heavy
my bed is bathed in tears
but when the night has ended
and I see the light again
I will keep on searching
for just one true friend.

GREAT GOD

My God is an awesome God
The great Warrior of all days
I'll love Him
serve Him honor
and give Him all my praise
The Creator of the universe
beginning and the end
He loves protects defends
and is my perfect friend
He sent His holy Son
A salvation from eternal strife
I want to give Him all I have
to Him I give my life.

RIP

Here he lies within his grave
to tawdry society he was a slave
never used the gifts God gave
and sadly now in death he lays
aimless
purposeless
callow
vapid
these words defined him well
and now his story has ended
a story
no one cares to tell.

MY SOULLESS WALKS

My soulless walks
on shattered words
that frame
an empty mind
and all I ever
thought or knew
has gone
and left me blind
I search down in
the darkest hole
deep within
an empty soul
to try reclaim
and take control
before the sun will rise
for soon
the morning breaks
and then
I face
my own demise.

LOST WITHOUT YOUR LOVE

I walk alone
down the lonely road
please hold my hand
in this darkness
the angel of death surrounds me
I am powerless without your love
the raging fires atop the mountain
spreads its death to the outer world
kiss me before my soul is lost
and I flounder in this living hell
I am lost without your love.

ETERNAL SHEETS

With you I'd tear
the eternal sheets
as we breathe forever
in a single heartbeat.

MY BESTEST FRIEND

Here on earth you're my best friend
I will always love you
until the very end
you are always there
in joy in loss
never thinking
of the cost
your spirit lifts me
when I'm down
your perfect smile
replaces my frown
these twenty years
have flown too fast
the memories
I hope will last
I love the times we cry and laugh
you always see my better half
you're beautiful in all the ways
the times we spent I miss those days
on that day when you must leave
your heart to someone give
I pray you find sweet happiness
a hundred years to live
no matter where you go in life
from start and to the end
you have my blessings and my love
you are my bestest friend.

MIND
In my mind in distant past
the time has come
realize at last
I enter in my blackest hole
to clear my mind emp
ty my soul
cold and sick black hole is deep
vitals have stopped
I enter sleep
within this place
my mind is free
for in this place I'm truly me.

BED

You haven't left my mind
since we parted this morning
my thoughts are on you
and they all are adoring
thoughts of tonight have me soaring
for happy times
when we'll be together again
I can't wait to be in you my friend
as my head lands on you then
dead
asleep
my beautiful bed.

ACE REPLACED

The music whispers
chimes will play
the shy turns red
it's yesterday
tomorrow's gone
the future past
next week is here
it did not last
the dice are rolled
the wars are hard
the moving stops
an extra card
the deck is cut
it only stares
a coffin shuts but no one cares
the sky is blood when it was black
and ace is gone replaced with jack
the sun is blind it's freezing cold
something new is something old
the music whispers
chimes will play
I don't exist
till yesterday.

DAEH

My heart is broken I hear the song
it's over now but what went wrong
time is short and minutes pass
I never dreamed it would not last
a silent voice still in me cries
I stand there helpless while he dies
the hand still holds
I can't let go
instead I laugh
so pain won't show
inside of me I'm on my knees
I try to reach but no one sees
the rain comes down it's freezing cold
I cannot feel
to dark my heart is sold
the picture changes into 3D
now there's two I'm watching me
I cannot help but feel the pain
uncaring faces without a name
joy is drowned in sorrow felt
while all that's good inside me melts
death is sure it's on the brink
my mind is still the missing link
another cliff another hump
I'm at the edge about to jump
is it real this place of dread
or just a place inside my head.

HUH?

The music plays
and so we walk
the music quits
and so we stop
a child dies
and no one cries
something gone
someone lies
a turbulent calm
screamed whisper said
a twisted thought
now someone's dead
a drop of ink
a piece of lead
it all takes place
inside my head.

MY PARTNER

Life's got me thinkin'
about the long road ahead
my one and only partner
was alive but now he's dead
we were just together
my partner and me
but now
he is dead and gone
how I wish it wouldn't be
we loved each other more than life
my partner and I
oh how I miss him
why did he have to die
we had life a runnin'
oh it was so fun
but now it all is over now
our time together has run.

MY BOY

I watch my little boy
a man some day he'll be
but my little boy
wants to grow
to be just like me
he watches me in all I do
he's watching all day long
and in his eyes I'm perfect
I can't yet do any wrong
I have to be all I can
and walk the narrow way
because soon my little boy will be
just like me one day
I love my little boy
he's everything to me
love hope and purity
all in him I see
so everyday
I strive to be
the best that I can be
in case my little boy
grows up to be like me.

PUPPET CLOWN

There's a road we all gotta walk down
and really ain't no telling
when we're puppeteer
or puppet clown
things we thought would bring a smile
sometimes bring a frown
and seeming acts of random
can flip it upside down.
empathy we should have more of
a lot more talking
and a lot less push and shove
remember God is watching
and we could all stand to
give a little more love.

CRYING SOUL

When my soul is crying
who hears?
is it only me
alone with my fears?
is it you who heals my heart
or you who makes me afraid of the dark
though I traversed a thousand trails
my love to you
saw no avail
a sealess ship
a shipless sail
save the words my love
they're too used to sell
I wish you love
just know for me it's hell
but until that time
I wish you love
I wish you well
and so saying
I screeching bid you farewell.

CRY TO GOD

I cry to God
please take my fears
I cry to him
please dry my tears
God I am so low
my ways my wants
only you can know
please cleanse my heart
it is so dark
please Lord come
and fill my heart
without you Lord
I'm nothingness
I'm Emptiness
without you Lord
in my Life I want you adored
I try to do it on my own
God I need you to arrive at home
each time I try
I fall short
without you Lord
I've bad report
revive me Lord
please cleanse my way
Lord God Yeshua please
I pray today.

FELLOWMAN

Why is the world so dark and cold
why does death take both young and the old
why is there sadness depression and fears
homeless and children drowning in tears
why the uncaring as the world passes by
not taking their time to comfort who cry
why the cold hearts who choose not to care
and leave little children alone standing there
the question is asked but no answers found
the world crying out yet we hear not a sound
the answer is people who selflessly give
their time and their money so others may live
there are the homeless who need only love
the weak and the low to get help from above
if we don't care and let them pass by
we'll realize the damage when it's our turn to die
to look on our past and see what needed done
instead of just caring for money and fun
now we must act and give all we can
one world together one fellow man.

POETRY
Poetry is song from the soul
and medicine for the heart
mind body and spirit
poetry comprises all parts
poetry is more than words
more than a melody
when normal words can't say how you feel
poetry helps them see
poetry will speak to you
it's a message all in itself
so next time that you see a poem
take it off the shelf
for when you read the pages
the words will speak to you
and no matter how much you read it
you will always find something new.

LIFE

Life may or may not be
all that it seems
a bright ray of hope
or just shattered dreams
something to look for
something to lose
filled with great findings
laced with bad news
there are lives we love
perhaps others we hate
some we almost barely just appreciate
so is it all just black and white
or the gray in-between?
so why do we live?
I mean what is life
besides joy and happiness
or bickering and strife?
I've pondered this question over again
but to my asking is there an end?
perhaps life's what we make it
as we live our lives each day
whether good or bad we all have a say
so with each new day
we must all do our best
do what we can
and let God do the rest.

FILL ME

The raindrops fall upon a flower
gentle rain begins to shower
and as the rain
will water the earth
Lord let your spirit
please quench my thirst
I long to know you
be by your side
Lord in my Heart
only you abide
You are the mighty
King of all
please let your grace
upon me fall
until I see you on that day
Lord fill my spirit
Lord I pray.

IF IT WAS LOVE

If it was love
how can I be expected
to say goodbye?
if it's true love I can't
shan't
won't
and
don't
surely
if it's love
I can't say a forever goodbye
because
true love
lives forever
in my happy
sad blue sky.

MISSING HIM
I miss him.
Always have
and I always will
each breath I draw
I miss him
more still.

A PAIN EXISTS

There exists a pain
time cannot heal
hurt as long as life
you will forever feel
those who deny
don't know that they lie
it's just their soulmate
has yet to die.

SIMPLE TRUTH
I can't stand the noise
crass poise
but I don't want to live in silence
so I play with their toys.

MISSIN' YOU

I spent the day in the garden
thinking of you
the sky was blue
beautiful California weather
nothing new
unless by new
another shade of missing you
the tea is ready
I've gotta go
but just so you know
I'm always thinking of you.

OUT THERE

I don't really got any good advice
but the way I see it
it's either lull or mental man
riding the gnarly waves
or rocks and ankle slappers
always feeling outgunned
and sure yeah
we all wanna hang ten
on a perfect barrel carve
and maybe we do
and that's friggin rad bro right
but if all we ever do
is go over the falls
we gotta know
in our soul we gotta know
it was just about being out there
just being out there is enough
even if we never win a hand bro
we got to play.

ALPHABET CAPER

Yesterday I went to the paper
and asked the letters to dance
in giddy romance
we got lost in a trance
magnifical
alphabet caper
but today when I went
all my partner's seemed spent
and I spent more time
with the eraser.

DEAR UNCLE DAVE

Heaven just got a whole lot sweeter
now that uncle Dave has flown away
to the celestial beyond
where all believers meet one day
our hearts are broken
tears are fresh
because a great light has gone
but the love of Yeshua
that lived in uncle Dave
is a Light that forever lives on
I haven't found the right words to say
with power to heal searing pain
in fact when I try
it sounds like a lie
and the wake leaves me feeling disdain
but if we love as he loved
the lost we can save
if we give as he gave
as his light we carry
from such a beautiful soul
dear fun uncle Dave
still reeling from the blow
of losing such a wonderful guy
and I'm sure I'll still ask God why
but I take comfort in knowing
I'll see him again
in the sweet by and by.

RAMBLES

Hello
once stranger now friend
do my dreams live in words
or action?
what are you life
you beautiful
mad-multi-faced
fast slow paced
reminded erased
magnificent
defiling
beguiling
tears fall smiling
wild thing
what sorrowful joy
to live you
as living brings
such a twisted song to sing.

A PRAYER

Dear God please
play my cello strings
your messenger of love let me be
your good tidings pray I bring
the hope of your love I cling
please let me paint the skies you see
pray let it not solemn be
but please let it be a reflection
of the joy you bring to me.

FLAME

To understand me
is knowing my flame
the fire I follow
even if it defames my "name"
for I believe it's the key
to life's twisted 'game'
learning to love
all souls the same
which isn't to say
mistakes I won't make
for I do
and I will
and so my actions
good or ill
I will always bare blame
in the chase towards perfection
it's on goodness I aim
try overcoming evil
my demons try change
which isn't to say I forget any shame
for mistakes live to teach me
so I must never declaim
as I travel this earthly plane
to know me truly
is to know my flame.

SUNKEN CANOE

Stuck between
everything's alright
and nothing's okay
where it's so hard to breathe
because I can't leave
but don't want to stay
try to take flight
with wings that are burned
saddled with a darkness
from all that I've learned
with a soul that's been spurned
as a stranger in my own home
and not to bemoan
but I'm surrounded by family
and still feel all alone
as a mangy street dog
scrounging trash for a bone
on choppy seas
with a shattered canoe
fully prone
to refusing to float
loves to sink
sinking sinking
like my joy and my hope
there's no rope no helping hand
just myself me and I man
seems the only three who give a damn.

THE COST
Who?
Her?
yeah
no I do NOT
"count the cost"
...okay I lie
I did
and without her
I'm surely lost.

NAKED THERE

Naked there I witnessed
bathed in blood
the giant of fear
her laughing
making ash
of that I hold
and hold so dear
hear the death voice
painful screaming
nightmare dreaming
pleading I should run
but my soul cannot be saved
so death I choose
let's have some fun
words I now shall cease
and fight we shall
to answer
the colors you've shown
it's war no dual
I'm not alone
fearing not your
evil demons legion
for we have brought our own.

LONELY VOID

You're in the lonely
dismal blackened void
I am here also
you can hear me in the darkness
walk towards the sound of my love
feel for my heartbeat
I am here
clasping your hand in mind
and though I cannot save you
in this darkness we can tarry together.

EIGHTY EIGHT

Love the song
listen to it
all night long
but I don't remember
when I lost my mind
memories are often
unkind
sometime in February
nineteen eighty eight
moments after being birthed
into this fate
eyes open
can relate
whispers
between the chalk
and the slate
all different nails
in the same crate
in a life
too advanced for checkers
because it's checkmate
bowl of fishes
pretending we ain't the bait
striving to love
because to drown is to hate.

IMAGINATION

As we flew thousands of feet above
I spied a light out my window
and wondered if it was you
perhaps you were in a majestic
magical
angelic plane
next to mine
going the opposite way
as we usually did
same journey different directions
how much I miss you
every moment of every day
memories must suffice
as little Ada would say
let's play imagination.

FEELING

I saw her again
I saw her today
if it isn't love
why's it hurt this way
I wish to never see her again
but then
I don't wish that today
I do and I don't
don't think about her
I will
I won't.

THE FATHERS LOVE

How deep the Father's love for us
how vast beyond all measure
that He should give His only Son
to make a wretch His treasure
how great the pain of searing loss
The Father turns His face away
as wounds which mar the Chosen One
bring many sons to glory
behold the man upon a cross
my sin upon His shoulders
ashamed
I hear my mocking voice
call out among the scoffers
it was my sin that held Him there
until it was accomplished
His dying breath has brought me life
I know that it is finished
I will not boast in anything
no gifts
no power no wisdom
but I will boast in Yeshua
His death and resurrection
why should I gain from His reward?
I cannot give an answer
but this I know with all my heart
His wounds have paid my ransom.

OLD SELF

Hello old self its me again
the same old different you
with the same old worn out name
we've known each other
as long as we've known
how many of us
I'm still unsure
there are moments I see so clearly
but most others just a blur
my presence has purpose
a question to you I pose
how am I supposed to love you
when you screw me wherever I go?
together we're stuck forever
and hate erodes body and soul
I only wish that over you
I had a little more control
you've embarrassed me in public
so I shame you in private
our endless tussle
lost in the hustle
never met another quite like it
never alone
in the sunshine or dark
caught between a little lamb
and a bloodthirsty poisonous shark.

NATURE

No thought of whisper
I dare not move or speak
I'm listening to nature
for the wisdom that I seek
all alone with nature
I can hear her all around
close my eyelids slowly to her sound
the graceful deer moves slowly
as the birds sing soft their song
the river though so powerful
flows gently all along
the wisdom nature gives me
is the peace in which she lies
serenity and happiness
betwixt the earth and skies
away from man and fighting
lose thought of pain and strife
to fall asleep with nature
rejuvenates new life
I feel myself sink slowly
and fade into the ground
as I'm one with nature
lost within her sound
the grass the wind blows gently
sun shining from above
and as I'm one with nature
all I feel is love.

LORD I PRAY

The rain begins to shower
droplets upon the flowers
and as the rain
waters the earth
Lord let your spirit
please quench my thirst
I long to know you
be by your side
Lord in my heart
pray only you abide
you are the mighty
King of all
please let your grace upon me fall
until I see you on that day
Lord fill my spirit
Lord,
this I pray.

THE RIVER
There is this little river
which I hold very dear
it's filled with all my trials
my worries and my fears
the river flows forever
and always in its place
to help me
and to guide me
as I traverse this maniacal space
the river always listens
to what I have to say
but now I'm brokenhearted
because it wasn't there today.

OPERATION TRYST

A private romantic rendezvous between lovers
the trystiest tryst
that trysted above all others
is you my darling love
it's you
you you you you you you you
you burn me with your passion
like walking barefoot on the sun
my calming seas and soulmate
the one and only one
you're the queen of all queens
the queen of my night
the queen of my light
the queen of my right
you dispel my ill spite
your love is my strength
the fire in my fight
Lady fairer than fair
eternal starlight
I love you I love you I love you
I love you with all of my might.

POST SHOUT

Soo as it turns out
today's the day
I always knew would come
in pain I am penning
though the lyrics sound fun
my lover loves her coffee
three minutes microwave
I've acquired a taste
so it too I crave
and together we drink
many many a day
two cups at a time
both the same way
well not every day because
she always drinks black
whereas I'm known to indulge
in a sugar cream heart attack
so today like most days
I went through
the motions
but wobbled the cup
rocking the ocean
tut tut
making today the day
speculated to come
I burned myself with my coffee
and it was no fun.

LOVE POTION
If our love were a fire
it would melt the universe
our unity as a potion
would dissolve any curse.

WORDS IN MY HEAD

I feel I'm going crazy
from the words in my head
but I'd be lonely without them
these words in my head
so I thank God above
for without them
I'd be dead.'

FUTURE MAKE

The past was ours to make
only us we can break
as the present be ours to quake
for the future is ours to take.

UNBLEACHED

Up in the DFAC
doling out food
feigning the advances
without being rude
another officer asks
What's your favorite flower?
unbleached
she smiled sweetly
not meaning to be dour.

<u>**MISTER SINISTER**</u>
When you've rambled as much as me
you're bound to feel alone
built so many houses
y'know it's hard
to know where's home
so lost in the night ever black
through the door so dark
it could only be opened
by the key from a broken heart
I'm bleedin' our my soul man
I'm bleeding it dry
cry why
why cry
cry why
and can't see one fool
who gives a damn
I'm the ghost man
the barren land
don't know who I am
except unless I'm the ghost man
the unplanned
if indeed I be the ghost man
come out of the closet
mister sinister
evil monster man
I didn't ask to play biggest sinner
but you my friend are damned.

WALK IT ONTO THE PAGE

When your heart's broken
walk it onto the page
let the lead and ink
scream out
the painful laughing
twisted
bloody rage.

INHERENT VICE

I wonder if my verses
will sail the sands of time
or just inherent vice
be empty words that rhyme.

INSIDE MY HEAD
I know a lot of people
they live inside my head
and I know they all will love you
until I and they are dead.

PAIR OF EYES

Since I can't be anyone but me
only got my own eyes
and they see what they see
then how do I know
'tis not a bush that I see
when thou sayest
not a bush but a tree.

SILVER AND KNOWLEDGE

Doth not wisdom cry?
and understanding put forth Her voice?
do we not have ears to hear
and free will to make the choice?
the fear of the LORD is to hate evil:
pride and arrogancy
and the evil way
and the froward mouth do I hate
for narrow is the way
and strait is the gate
because
the LORD possessed me
in the beginning of His way
since before the first day
before His works of old
then and now
my soul He shall hold for
eternity beyond body gone cold
blessed He
King of Kings
Lord of wisdom riches untold.

PORT
I knew a lot of people
but none I felt were home
and then you came along
to show
I ain't gotta walk alone.

SWEETER'N SWEET TEA

You're sweeter than the sweetest sweet tea
more than the honey from the honey bee
more oxygen than from atop the tallest tree
and even with theses words
I can't explain how much
you mean to me
'cuz you're my favorite pie
the answer to why
the angel that holds me when I cry
boy I love you
my message is true
we're both cloudy
but we make our sky blue.

<u>*VERY EXTREMELY PRETTY*</u>
You told me
someone told you
you were ugly
and well I say they're wrong
you're very extremely pretty
and I think about you
all day and night long.

WORDS

We know that words
don't write themselves
and empty books
should never occupy shelves
so I pray ore the paper
I be lit with literary caper
ambition not taper
as I endeavor
to create
an honest soul shape
letter verse fully free
no matter how sad dramatic
or tee hee comedy.

THE MADDENING HIVE
Some thrive
in the maddening hive
most barely survive
but none get out alive.

MORE THAN WINDS BLOW

I love you
more than the wind can blow
more than any human will ever know
from summer's sun to winters snow
more than I can possibly show
so much so
I hope you know
my love for you will only grow
my lovely love
my love my love
from heart to soul
to head to toe
may it blow
may it grow
may it forever show
and may all know know
know know know
I love I love I love
I love I love I love
I love I love I love
and so to you I go.

INK AND QUIRE
My mortar and pestle
are ink and quire
to expel my
disdain and desire
on paths of dirt
and streets of gold
joy and hurt
mountains and mire
tales new and old
the fingers flit
under moon and sun
scribing the story
that's never done.

LITTLE ANNA MARIE

My baby girl named Anna Marie
was six and a half years old
and she meant so much more to me
than all the earthly gold
I remember when she was born
the new meaning to life she gave
it was then I was hers forever
my heart to hers was slave
she was so full of life and promise
so sweet so loving and kind
she never seemed to care about
that she had been born blind
she told me once when she was five
with childlike faith and love
she was happy the first faces she would see
were God's and the angels above
when she was born
her mother left us
to walk through life alone
but I never ever minded
that she was all my own
she taught me so much
about this life
far beyond her years
how to truly feel at peace
and how to quell my fears
I always cooked her favorite meals

and sang her to sleep at night
my precious little angel
so full of life and light
a year ago it was her and I
playing ball on the grass
the phone rang and I told her
hold on I'll be right back
I never knew what happened
the neighbors didn't see
all I know
is Anna Marie
is no longer with me
I wrote letters
searched and looked
the police could find no trace
all I'm left with now are memories
of her precious little face
I always cook her favorite meal
and every day is night
I lost my little angel
I lost my guiding light
I cry to God throughout the day
and dream of her at night
I'll look for her forever
with promise as my sight
I sorry baby I failed you
and crushed your love and faith
for my soul I have nothing

but contempt and hate
please dear God I'm begging you
to take my life tonight
that is the price I want to pay
if it means my baby's alright
I love you little Anna Marie
I love you so
so much
I miss your little hand in mine
to feel our fingers touch
don't think about forgiving me
for my soul there is none
for on that day I let you go
my heart and soul were done
now I'm sobbing and begging to God
just bring you safely back to me
I love you my little angel
my darling Anna Marie.

JACK AND JILL
Now I know
why Jack fell down the hill
he was head over heels
for Jill.

HAPPY WRITING
Happy writing to thee
and your story
fighting to be free
write until it's writ
don't let them fingers quit.

...let the poetry show it to thee.

Write your verse.

Write your verse.

Write your verse.

Write your verse.

Write your verse.

Write your verse.

Write your verse.

Write your verse.

In Friendship Love and Truth.
-Josiah Jack

Made in the USA
Middletown, DE
13 November 2024